This edition first published in the United States in 2003 by MONDO Publishing, by arrangement with Siphano Picture Books, Ltd., London. Text and illustrations © 2002 by Siphano Picture Books, Ltd., London

For information contact:
MONDO Publishing
980 Avenue of the Americas
New York, NY 10018
Please visit our web site at http://www.mondopub.com
Color separation by Vivliosynergatiki, Athens, Greece
Printed in Italy by Grafiche AZ, Verona
First MONDO printing September 2003
ISBN 1-59034-582-7(hardcover)   ISBN 1-59034-583-5 (pbk.)
03 04 05 06 07 08 09 HC 9 8 7 6 5 4 3 2 1
03 04 05 06 07 08 09 PB 9 8 7 6 5 4 3 2 1
Originally published in London in 2002 by Siphano Picture Books, Ltd.
Typesetting and design for this edition by Edward Miller

Library of Congress Cataloging-in-Publication Data
Bloom, Becky,
    Leo and Lester / by Becky Bloom ; illustrated by Pascal Biet. -- 1st U. S. ed.
        p cm
 Summary: When Leo the raccoon and Lester the hippopotamus go to town, Leo has the challenging job of monitoring Lester's manners.
ISBN 1-59034-582-7 (hc.) -- ISBN 1-59034-583-5 (pbk.)
 [1. Manners and customs--Fiction. 2. Behavior--Fiction. 3. Raccoons--Fiction. 4. Hippopotamus--Fiction.] I. Biet, Pascal, ill. II. Title.

PZ7.B62275 Le 2003
[E] -- dc21

                                                           2002033778

Leo and Lester

by Becky Bloom • Illustrated by Pascal Biet

MONDO

Lester and his friend Leo were going into town together.

"Please be careful, Lester," said his grandmother. "And try to be considerate to others."

"Of course!" said Lester. "I always know how to behave. Listen:

PLEASE may I have my hat, Grandma.

THANK YOU, Grandma!

EXCUSE ME, Grandma!"

"There's more to good manners than saying 'Please,' 'Thank You,' and 'Excuse Me,' Lester," said Grandmother. "Why not let Leo help you brush up on your manners?"

So Leo agreed to give Lester some lessons.

Don't block
the escalator—
stand
to one side.

Litter goes in the
garbage can, not on
the ground!

LESSON 1
AROUND TOWN

When you're shopping, put things you don't want back on the shelf.

Always let others off of the bus before you try to get on.

"Don't worry," said Lester after the lesson was over. "I always behave when I'm in town!"

When they had finished their shopping, Lester decided to try out his new skateboard.

"NO LESTER—not with the shopping bags!" cried Leo.

Too late! The skateboard slid in a puddle and Lester crashed into some people passing by. What a mess! They all fell down, groceries went flying, and so did Lester's bag of socks, a new pack of baseball cards, and his hat and sunglasses. Mr. Cat got the skateboard in his face and Rabbit lost his ice cream cone . . .

. . . most of which
landed on Leo's head.

Lester said "Please," "Thank You," and
"Excuse Me," but it didn't help.

Leo was very embarrassed and started
to clean up Rabbit.

Meanwhile, all this skateboarding and splashing
was making Lester feel hungry . . . .

LESSON 2:
EATING OUT

Always wash your hands
before eating.

Knives, forks, and spoons
are for eating—not
for playing drums
on the table!

t OR talk—
do not try to
oth at the
e time!

"Don't worry," said Lester after the lesson.
"I always behave in restaurants."

Their food took some time
to arrive. Lester started blowing
bubbles in his soda . . .

and when lunch did come,
he gobbled it down and built
a tower with his leftovers . . .

and when the tower fell over,
his cup fell on the floor and he
crawled under the table to get it . . . .

"NO, LESTER!" cried Leo.
"You don't fit!"

Too late! The table tipped over,
and food flew everywhere.

Lester said
"Please," "Thank You," and
"Excuse Me," but it didn't help. The waiter said he
never wanted to see them in the restaurant again.

Leo said "Sorry" to everyone.

By now, Lester was thinking about going to the park . . . .

Remember to skate on the paved path and not in the flower beds.

The plants and flowers are for everyone—so don't pick them!

16

Do feed the ducks—
but only if
it is allowed!

Don't play loud
music—others may
not like it.

"Don't worry," said Lester after the lesson. "I *always* behave in the park!"

But when he started playing soccer, he kicked the ball straight into the foxes' picnic!

And when he flew his kite, he tried to do some tricks . . . .

"CAREFUL, LESTER!" cried Leo. "Watch out for the sandcastle!"

Too late! Lester got tangled in the kite string and tripped. He fell headfirst into the sandbox, squashing the sandcastle flat.

Lester said "Please," "Thank You," and "Excuse Me,"
but it didn't help. "I'm so sorry," he added—copying what
Leo said—but that didn't help much, either.

Leo decided they should visit their friend
Mr. Alligator. A visit would keep Lester inside
and hopefully out of trouble . . . .

20

"Don't worry," said Lester.
"I always behave in friends' houses."
But he was feeling thirsty, so he opened the refrigerator without asking, slurped down all the milk, and spilled some of it on the floor . . .

then he knocked over a very nice lamp . . .

and when he saw an interesting book on the shelf, he grabbed it and knocked some other books down, right onto Mr. Alligator's head!

Then Lester tried to be helpful. But as he carried out a tray of fruit juice, he showed off his silly walk—and juice spilled everywhere!

Lester said "Please," "Thank You," and "Excuse Me," but it didn't help at all. Then he offered to clean up, and everyone thought that was very nice of him. Leo was pleased, too. He didn't have to apologize for Lester this time!

By now it was getting late—time for Leo and Lester to go home . . . .

Always put your clothes away.

29

"Don't worry," said Lester after the lesson. "I *always* behave well at home."

In the living room, he took all his toys out and scattered them everywhere. He played his music so loudly it gave Leo a headache.

When Lester decided to watch a movie, his sandwich nearly got put into the VCR!

"Let's have some of Grandma's raspberry pie," said Lester. He took a big slice and left the rest on the sofa.

Leo then sat down— on the raspberry pie!

"Lester," cried Leo, "that's ENOUGH! We must clean up this mess . . . NOW!"

"I'll clean up," said Lester. "You have a rest."

Without so much as a "Please," "Thank You," or "Excuse Me," Lester picked things up and put them away, then swept, wiped, and scrubbed.

"My, my . . . what a clean house!" said Grandmother, when she came back from shopping. "Lester, you have behaved yourself!"

"Thanks to Leo's lessons," said Lester. "Well . . . I suppose I did make one or two mistakes . . . but tomorrow I will be on my very best behavior!"